Chase is Ready for Takeoff

Written by: Cousin John
Illustrated by: Catienna Regis

This book is dedicated to Chase & Emerson.

Chase woke up nervous, and his palms
were sweaty.

A trip was planned for Chase and his mom, but he
just wasn't ready.

His suitcase was packed and it was time to go.

But there was just one thing that he wanted
to know.

Chase asked his mom, "Why can't we take a bus or a train?"

That's when she realized he was scared to fly on a plane.

Chase finally told his mom about his big fear.

"Don't worry," she said with a smile from ear to ear.

They boarded the plane on their way to Los Angeles.

Chase thought to himself, "I don't think I can handle this."

That's when a flight attendant walked down the aisle.

Her name was Ann, and she had a great big smile.

She asked Chase if this was his first flight.

He nodded his head yes, and asked if he should hold on tight.

She told him there was nothing to worry about, and he should enjoy the ride.

"Look at the bright side," she said. "All the beautiful clouds are right next to you in the sky?"

It was time for takeoff, and the plane rolled down the runway.

Chase knew if he could get through this part, it would be a fun day.

Before he could panic the plane had taken off.

Chase realized the flight attendant was right. The clouds looked so fluffy and soft.

Chase and his mom had a great time in Los Angeles once they got off the plane.

They saw palm trees everywhere and even went to a Lakers game.

They went to Long Beach and enjoyed a quick swim.

Chase wished he could go to Roscoe's for chicken and waffles again.

But it was time to go explore a new space.

Off to the airport they went to travel to a beautiful place.

Chase was excited that he was going to Paris.

But he was scared to get on another plane and felt embarrassed.

On the plane, Chase met a tall man in a suit that was blue.

"Excuse me sir," said Chase. "Are you going to Paris too?"

"Of course. It's my job to get you there," the man in blue explained.

The man in the suit was the pilot. He's the person who actually flies the plane.

The pilot told Chase that an airplane is just like a bird. They both have wings.

The only difference is that airplanes take people to see amazing things.

Chase slid down in his seat, all out of excuses.

He thought to himself, "I don't think I can do this."

Just when Chase was about to panic, a familiar face showed up.

His friend Jay from school was in the seat behind him, drinking orange juice out of a cup.

Jay was sitting in his seat, as comfortable as can be.

"I used to be scared too," said Jay. "But now flying is fun to me."

Jay had an idea that would help his friend.

The two boys pretended to be super heroes until the flight came to an end.

On the first flight Chase was so nervous that he squeezed his mom's hand.

Now Chase was having so much fun, that he didn't realize it was time to land.

Now that they were in Paris, Chase and his mom were ready for a great time.

They explored museums and ate pasta while enjoying the sunshine.

As much fun as they were having in Paris, Chase and his mom had one more stop.

It was time to get on another plane, to visit Chase's grandpop.

Chase knew Grandpop Herb lived somewhere near a beach.

Last time he was there, he saw more boats in the water than cars on the street.

Chase's mom pulled out her phone and pointed to where they were going on a map.

They had a long flight to Hawaii, and she told Chase he should take a nap.

Chase started to get scared again, but then he looked around.

Everyone on the plane was asleep, and snores from the passengers was the only sound.

He thought to himself, "If everyone is calm enough to sleep then there's no need to worry."

But as soon as the plane landed, Chase was ready to hop off in a hurry.

Going to Hawaii was like a trip to the zoo.

There were dolphins, turtles and fish that would swim right up to you.

"Chase, I have a surprise for you," said Grandpop Herb with a smirk.

"Today, your cousin Emy is going to teach you how to surf!"

It was a struggle at first, but Chase never gave up.

"It's all about balance," said Emy. "Believe me it's tough."

Before long the practice began to pay off for Chase.

He was surfing the waves like a pro with so much grace.

The time in Hawaii was fun, but it was coming to an end.

Chase realized that he would have to get on an airplane once again.

His legs began to shake like the leaves on a tree.

But then Chase had a thought that put his mind at ease.

Airplanes helped Chase travel to very far places, and everyone was so polite.

The least he could do is say thank you, and wish them all a safe flight.

From the flight attendant to the pilot, they all made Chase feel better.

He decided to do something special, and write each person a thank you letter.

Chase came home and told everyone about his trip.

He had so many stories, but there was one part of vacation he could not skip.

"Traveling is fun," said Chase. "Everyone should try."

"Just remember, there's no need to be scared when it's time to fly."

About the Author

John Butler, known as Cousin John, is a Philadelphia native and sports journalist who has turned his passion for writing into a series of children's books, providing valuable lessons to young readers. To learn more about Cousin John and new releases, visit ChaseBooks.com.

Made in the USA
Monee, IL
06 December 2021